MW01114490

SACAJAWEA

Gloria D. Miklowitz

Dominie Press, Inc.

Publisher: Raymond Yuen
Editor: John S. F. Graham
Designer: Greg DiGenti
Illustrator: Mario Capaldi

Published by:

ㄹ Dominie Press, Inc.
1949 Kellogg Avenue
Carlsbad, California 92008 USA

www.dominie.com

Paperback ISBN 0-7685-1221-2
Library Bound Edition ISBN 0-7685-1546-7
Printed in Singapore by PH Productions Pte Ltd
  2 3 4 5 6 PH 04 03

Table of Contents

Chapter 1

A Token of Peace

In 1805, a teenage Shoshone girl went with Captain Meriweather Lewis and Lieutenant William Clark on their famous expedition through the Louisiana Territory. She served as an interpreter while Lewis and Clark searched for a land route through the Rocky Mountains to the Pacific Ocean.

*Meriweather Lewis, Toussaint Charbonneau,
and Sacajawea*

Imagine this: You are a twelve-year-old Shoshone Indian girl in the late 1700s. You have always lived in what is now Idaho with your family and friends. One day, gunfire and screams awaken you. The Hidatsa Indians from North Dakota are attacking. You run, but you are captured. For five years you live as a slave with the Hidatsa, far away from your own tribe. Then a French trapper named Toussaint Charbonneau "buys" you from them to be his wife.

Sacajawea was that girl. In Hidatsa, her name means "bird woman." She became an important addition to the Lewis and Clark expedition.

In May, 1804 Captain Lewis and fellow officer Clark, under orders from President Thomas Jefferson, left Illinois. They traveled by canoe up the Missouri river. Their purpose was to find a way through the newly acquired territory, called the Louisiana Purchase, and beyond, to the Pacific Ocean.

They reached what is now North Dakota in October and directed their men to build Fort Mandan in Hidatsa territory. During the winter months, they learned what they could about the course of the Missouri River and had supplies brought in. They also hired Charbonneau, Sacajawea's husband, to be an interpreter. Charbonneau spoke French and knew some Indian languages, but did not speak English. Both Lewis and Clark spoke only English. One of the men on the expedition knew French, so he translated for Lewis and Clark when they needed to get information from Charbonneau. He then spoke to

Sacajawea in a combination of French and Hidatsa, and she would answer in the same way.

When Lewis and Clark learned that she was a Shoshone Indian, they asked that Charbonneau take her along on their expedition. They thought she would be a valuable interpreter when they reached Shoshone territory. They also thought that being seen with an Indian woman would let other Indians know that their mission was peaceful. They wanted to avoid conflicts as much as possible. Clark wrote in his journal, "a woman with a party of men is a token of peace."*

The Lewis and Clark expedition left Fort Mandan on April 7, 1805. In

---

*There are excerpts from individual journals in this book. These excerpts are shown exactly as written, and often contain misspellings and poor grammar.

the canoes were 31 men, including
Charbonneau and Sacajawea, with her
two-month-old son, Jean Baptiste—
nicknamed "Pomp," which means "First
Born" in Hidatsa.

A very long journey by canoe, on
foot, and on horseback had begun.

Chapter 2

Bird Woman's River

As the canoes eased away from shore that day in April 1805, Sacajawea sat in the open sun at the bottom of the largest canoe. Her son, Pomp, was strapped into a cradle board on her back. Animal pelts, blankets, medical supplies, gunpowder canisters, and other precious equipment were stored around her. On a platform in back of the canoe sat Lewis and Clark, protected from the sun by an awning. Clark's servant, York, and Lewis's big dog, Seaman, were also in the canoe, along with the head boatman.

Little is known of Sacajawea's feelings. Was she afraid? Did she look forward to being among her own people again? All we know about her on this difficult journey comes from 15 entries in Lewis and Clark's journals, written in poor English.

The first entry in Clark's journal, on the day of departure, lists among those in the expedition: "Shabonah and his Indian squar... Sah-kah-gar-We-a." He spelled her name as he thought it sounded, with a "G," not a "J." The

Lweis and Clark's canoe, with
Sacajawea and her husband

Hidatsa did not have a written language
at the time, so he tried to spell it the
best he could. Various journal entries
spell her name in different ways, and
the name *Sacajawea* has been written
differently throughout history. Some
people spell it *Sacagawea* and others
spell it *Sakakawea*. In all the journal
entries, there is no description of what
she looked like.

Two days out of Fort Mandan, Clark wrote, "The squaw busied herself in searching for the wild artichokes... she procured a good quantity of these roots."

More than once the journals mention Sacajawea's knowledge of edible berries, roots, and plants, which she collected for food and medicinal use. Clark wrote that these "add much to the comfort of our diet."

A month and a half into the trip, perhaps from gratitude for her usefulness, Lewis named a river's tributary after her, calling it *Sah-ca-gah-we-ah*, meaning *Bird Woman's River*. This was the first of many mountain peaks, lakes, parks, monuments, and markers named in her honor in the years to come.

Chapter 3

Quick and Clear-thinking

On May 14, 1805, the lead canoe, with Lewis, Clark, and Sacajawea, hit rough water. Charbonneau, who was at the tiller, did not handle the steering well, and the canoe nearly tipped over. In the resulting commotion, many essential supplies washed overboard. Quick and clear-thinking Sacajawea, in the rear of the canoe, quickly retrieved many of the scattered supplies back on board, including Clark's journal and valuable medicines.

A month later, Lewis wrote in his journal, "About two p.m. I reached the camp and found the Indian woman extremely ill and much reduced by her indisposition."

He went on to say that he cared for her and her young baby. He was concerned not only for her but also about the need they would have for her when they reached Shoshone territory. They were depending on her knowledge of Shoshone customs and language in order to communicate with them. They would need her help buying horses and other supplies to carry their canoes and equipment from the Missouri River over the Rocky Mountains and to the Columbia River.

Clark tried every medication he could think of to help her, but to no effect. Lewis, meanwhile, had been on a short exploring trip. On his return, he saw how sick she was. He said he passed a spring with mineral water on his trip and made a note of where it was. Sacajawea was treated with this water and recovered in a short time.

Later, camped below the great falls of the Missouri River, they could not go forward because the river was moving too fast. They had to carry their canoes and baggage beyond the treacherous rapids.

A rainstorm forces the explorers to get to higher ground

One day, a sudden rainstorm sent a wall of water rushing down the narrow canyon. The only escape was to get to high ground.

Clutching her son, Pomp, and getting help from Clark, Sacajawea scrambled up the nearly sheer, slippery rocks to the safety of the canyon rim.

Throughout the expedition, Indians watched the boats, but did not attack. Sometimes, the Indians befriended them. Sacajawea's presence made the difference. A woman and child would not be traveling with a war party.

And then, by amazing luck, Sacajawea started to recognize the landscape around them. They had reached Shoshone territory.

Chapter 4

Friend Embraced Friend

One morning, the expedition left a dangerous gorge and came out onto a wide plain. Three rivers met and joined to form the Missouri. Lewis and Clark named the rivers the Jefferson, the Madison, and the Gallatin. But they didn't know which one would take them into the mountains and to the source of the Missouri.

Sacajawea recognized landmarks from her old home. This was where her people, the Shoshone, had camped when they were attacked by the Hidatsa, almost five years earlier. Lewis wrote in his journal that she showed little emotion as she told about the raid and the deaths of the men, women, and children she had known.

Clark walked along the riverbank with her to see where the incidents had occurred. As they explored, she pointed to some oddly shaped mountains ahead. She said the Shoshone went there to collect red clay to paint their faces. Nearby was the mountain pass that led to her childhood home.

Captain Lewis was impatient to reach the Shoshone so he could buy horses and get over the mountains before snow fell. He left to search for a way through the pass with three other men. Clark and the rest of the group continued upriver.

It was cold, wet, and hard work pulling the canoes through shallow water and rapids. To lighten the load, Sacajawea walked along the bank carrying Pomp, with Clark and Charbonneau beside her.

Suddenly, they saw Indians on horseback and a crowd of women and children approaching. Sacajawea cried out and ran forward. They were her people! Friend embraced friend. Indians embraced Clark's men and gestured for them to follow to their camp.

Sacajawea greets her Shoshone family and friends

23

Leading the Shoshone was Chief Cameahwait, Sacajawea's brother. They had been separated for more than five years. She ran and threw her arms around him. As a gift, she gave him a lump of sugar, something he had never tasted. Pleased with the sight of his sister again and with her gift, he promised to help her companions.

Chapter 5

Patience, Good Nature, and Usefulness

Sacajawea arranged the purchase of horses at the Shoshone village. She also got her brother's promise to guide the explorers over the mountains.

One day, she learned that her brother intended to take a hunting party to find game instead. She warned Lewis. He called the chiefs together and reminded them of their promise. Cameahwait canceled the hunt.

By the time the expedition left the Shoshone, it was late August and the mountain passes were already snowy. Horses stumbled on the narrow, icy trails. One rolled down the hill with its load.

Snow and sleet fell. Hot weather followed cold, and many of the men got sick. Sacajawea not only helped the sick, but cared for her own child as well, who was by then seven months old.

Over the next few months, they struggled through rapids in canoes, traveled on land by horse or on foot, and finally reached the coast of Oregon. There they built Fort Clatsop, named for the Clatsop Indians who lived in the area. They decided to remain at the fort until spring, then start the journey back.

It was a period of almost constant rain. "O! How disagreeable is our Situation dureing the dreadful weather," Clark wrote.

While there, Lewis and Clark mapped their journey, studied the nearby Indian tribes and wrote in their journals. Sacajawea got to see the ocean—and one day got to see the remains of a whale on the beach.

On August 16, 1806, they arrived back at Fort Mandan. Clark credited Sacajawea for many qualities, especially her patience, good nature, and usefulness among the Shoshone.

After the expedition ended, Charbonneau received about $500 and plot of land as a thank you from the United States government. He, Sacajawea, and Pomp joined Clark in St. Louis. They hoped to make a life there, but Charbonneau missed the plains up north, the fur trading, and his friends. He and Sacajawea went back.

Sacajawea's life ended at a fur-trading outpost on the northern Missouri River. On December 10, 1812, a clerk at Fort Manuel wrote, "This evening the Wife of Charbonneau, a Snake Squaw, died of a putrid fever, she was a good and the best woman in the fort, age abt 25 years she left a fine infant girl." Eventually, Clark would adopt both of Sacajawea's children—the girl, named Lisette, and her brother, Pomp (Jean Baptiste)—in St. Louis.

Sacajawea is one of the most honored women in American history. There are many schools, parks, and other monuments named after her. In 2000, a gold-colored dollar coin showing Sacajawea with Pomp on her back was minted in her honor.

William Clark, with Jean-Baptiste (Pomp) and Lisette

Glossary

Acquired - got.

Arms - weapons.

Awning - a protective covering, usually made out of cloth or other material.

Canister - a small container.

Captain - in the army, the rank between Lieutenant and Major.

Commotion - activity, sometimes associated with being disorganized, like after an accident or disaster.

Customs - traditions; local practices. Sometimes known as unwritten rules.

Disagreeable - very uncomfortable. A disagreeable person can be difficult to get along with.

Edible - able to be eaten without making you sick.

Expedition - a journey with the purpose of discovering unknown lands.

Gallatin, Albert - the Secretary of the Treasury under Thomas Jefferson. He helped pay for Lewis and Clark's expedition.

Gorge - a narrow canyon with tall, steep walls.

Indisposition - inability to be useful; sick.

Interpreter - someone who knows more than one language in order to act as a go-between for two other people who do not speak the same language. see *Translate*

Markers - signs, plaques, or other objects that mark historical sites.

Outpost - an area in the wilderness where people can go to get supplies without having to travel to a city.

Pelts - animal skins, usually from small animals.

Precious - valuable; not easily replaced.

Putrid Fever - a disease caused by bacteria. Today, it is called *diphtheria*. It used to be a very common disease until a vaccine was developed. Now it is very rare.

Rapids - fast-moving parts of a river.

Snake - an old frontier term used to refer to Indians, sometimes just for Shoshone Indians.

Squaw - a old term used to refer to Indian women. Sometimes misspelled as *squar*.

Tiller - rudder of a small boat; used for turning.

Translate - to change from one language to another while keeping the same meaning. see *Interpreter*

Treacherous - dangerous, often associated with a journey or a trail.

Tributary - a small river that flows into a larger river.

Territory - region.

Pronunciation Guide

Toussaint Charbonneau: too - say' shar' - buh - noh'

Cameahwait: ka' - mee - ah - wait'

Clatsop: klat' - sahp

Gallatin: gahl - ah - tahn'

Hidatsa: hih - dat '- sah

Jean-Baptiste: zhon' - bahp - teest'

Lisette: lee - set'

Mandan: man' - dan

Meriweather: mare' - ih - weh' - ther

Sacagawea: sah' - kah - gah - wee' - ah

Sacajawea: sah' - kah - jah - wee '- ah

Shoshone: shoh - shoh' - nee